LOOK AND FIND®

Disney·PIXAR

MONSTERS, INC.

Illustrated by Art Mawhinney

Published by
Louis Weber, C.E.O.
Publications International, Ltd.
7373 North Cicero Avenue
Lincolnwood, Illinois 60712

www.pubint.com

Look and Find is a registered trademark of
Publications International, Ltd.

Manufactured in U.S.A.

8 7 6 5 4 3 2 1

ISBN 0-7853-5848-X

Publications International, Ltd.

Sulley and Mike are good citizens because they are walking to work to conserve scream energy. Maybe some of the other monsters should walk to work, too. There is a lot of traffic. Can you find these vehicles?

Mike's car

Snarley-Davidson

Yeller Cab

Octocycle

I-Scream Truck

Dragon Racer

Wretch Limo

Ghoulsmobile

Welcome to Monsters, Inc. Today is *Bring Your Little Monster to Work Day*, but things are not really *working* out that well. Lots of the kids are separated from their parents. Can you find and match each lost kid to the correct parent?

Tyler

Tiffany

Cole

Ashley

Brandon

Brittney

Jennifer

Alexander

This is the Scare Floor, and the monsters are preparing to scare. Everyone is trying to be very frightening, but even monsters need a little help sometimes. Can you find these scary things for the monsters to use?

Set of choppers

Extra eyeball

Suction snout

Pair of claw gloves

POP QUIZ

Pop quiz

Horn band

Tongue extension

Add-a-Tail

Randall is a very frightening monster, and he is proud of it. He can hide anywhere and use the element of surprise to scare kids. Can you find all the good hiding places in this poor kid's room?

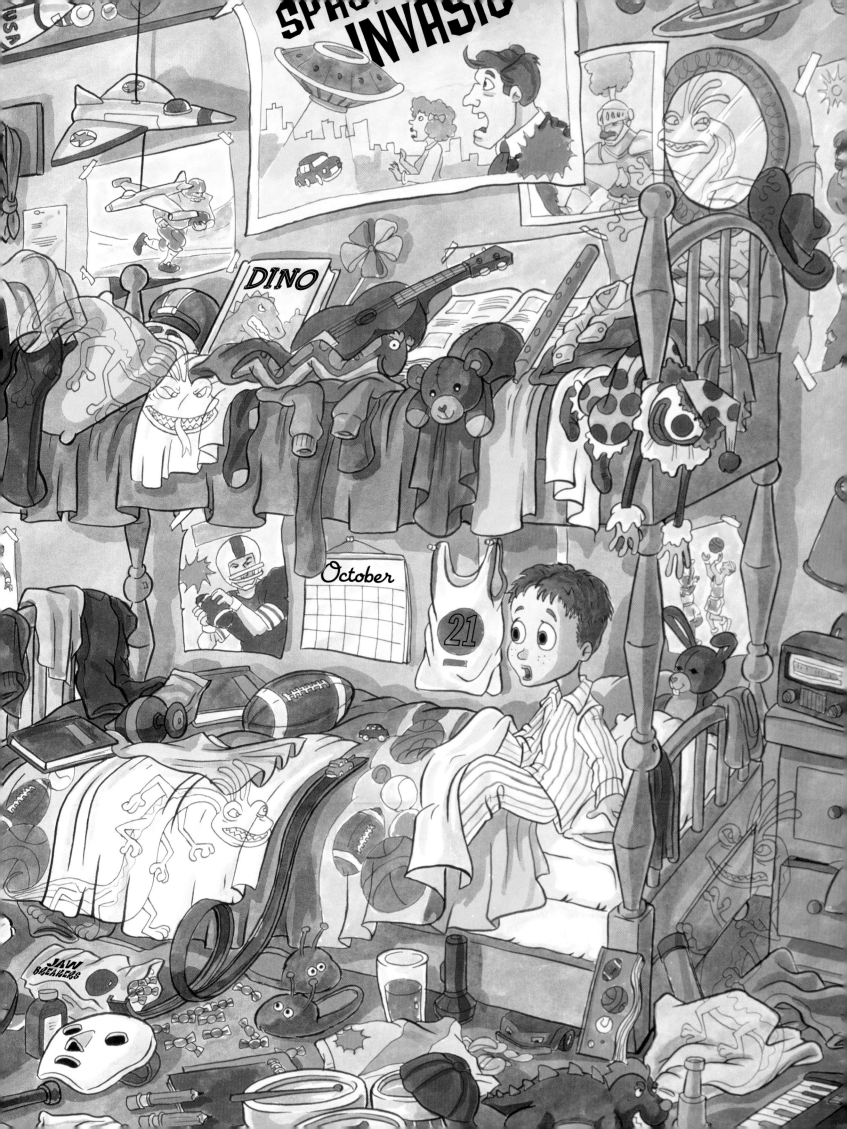

It's chaos at Harryhausen's. Boo may be small, but she is causing a lot of trouble. Everyone has seen her, and everyone is scared. Look for these very important monsters in the scene.

Mayor of Monstropolis

Miss Monstropolis

Anchorman

Fluffy Poodlepuff

Ellington Kingsley Poodlepuff, IV

Jean-Pierre LeScare

Major Catastrophe

Dr. Ringworm

Sulley and Mike manage to get Boo back to their apartment. They aren't quite sure what to do with her, but she seems to have her own ideas. She is contaminating all of Mike's stuff, and it is driving him crazy. Find Mike's *former* favorite things.

Sunglass

Book

Calendar

Mug

Chair

Teddy bear

Pizza box

Baseball cap

So many doors and so little time! Sulley and Mike don't know whether they are coming or going, but they must find Boo before Randall does. While you help them look, can you also find the closet doors that belong to these kids?

Boo

Jenna

Caleb

Tim

Louis

Rayna

Lily

Ginger

This is the new Laugh Floor, and the monsters are going about things a little differently. They are having lots of fun, but it is still hard work. Not everyone is a comedian. Lend a hand by finding these funny things for the monsters to use.

Squirting flower

Can of nuts

Whoopee cushion

Pie for throwing

Banana peel

Pair of funny glasses

Clown nose

Trick arrow

Sulley is a hero! Go back to Monstropolis to look for these items that celebrate Sulley.

___ A chalk drawing
___ A doll
___ A billboard
___ An autograph
___ A look-alike
___ A magazine cover
___ An ice sculpture
___ A T-shirt

It is Celia's birthday. Go back to Monsters, Inc., to look for these things that she will be receiving.

___ A birthday cake
___ A balloon
___ A bouquet of flowers
___ A singing telegram
___ A birthday card
___ A birthday present

Monsters are scared of human things. Go back to the Scare Floor to find some of the things that scare them.

___ A sock
___ A rubber ducky
___ A baseball cap
___ A dolly
___ A baseball glove
___ A bathing suit
___ A sneaker

Even familiar things can be scary in the dark. Go back to the kid's room to look for these creepy things.

___ A clown
___ A flying monkey
___ A man-eating plant
___ A bat
___ A pair of yellow eyes
___ An alien spaceship

No one is hungry anymore. Go back to Harryhausen's to find these things no one wants to eat.

_____ Key Slime Pie

_____ Eyeball Delight

_____ Stinky Futo Maki

_____ Garbage Salad

_____ String Beans

_____ Cream of Swamp Water Soup

_____ Sushi Under Glass

Human kids are picky! Go back to Sulley and Mike's apartment to find these things Boo wouldn't eat.

_____ A pickle

_____ A pizza

_____ An onion

_____ A tomato

_____ A sub sandwich

_____ An orange

_____ A can of spinach

Human kids put scary stuff on their closet doors! Go back to the chase scene to look for these scary things.

_____ A game of tic-tac-toe

_____ A chart of the solar system

_____ A picture of a clown

_____ A dart board

_____ A map of the world

_____ A calendar

_____ An A+ report

_____ A dinosaur painting

Laughter is the best energy! Go back to the Laugh Floor to find these silly monsters who make kids laugh.

_____ A monster in a bucket

_____ A ventriloquist monster

_____ A juggling monster

_____ An upside-down monster

_____ A tutu-wearing monster

_____ A tap-dancing monster

_____ A shadow-puppet monster

_____ A trick-photographer monster

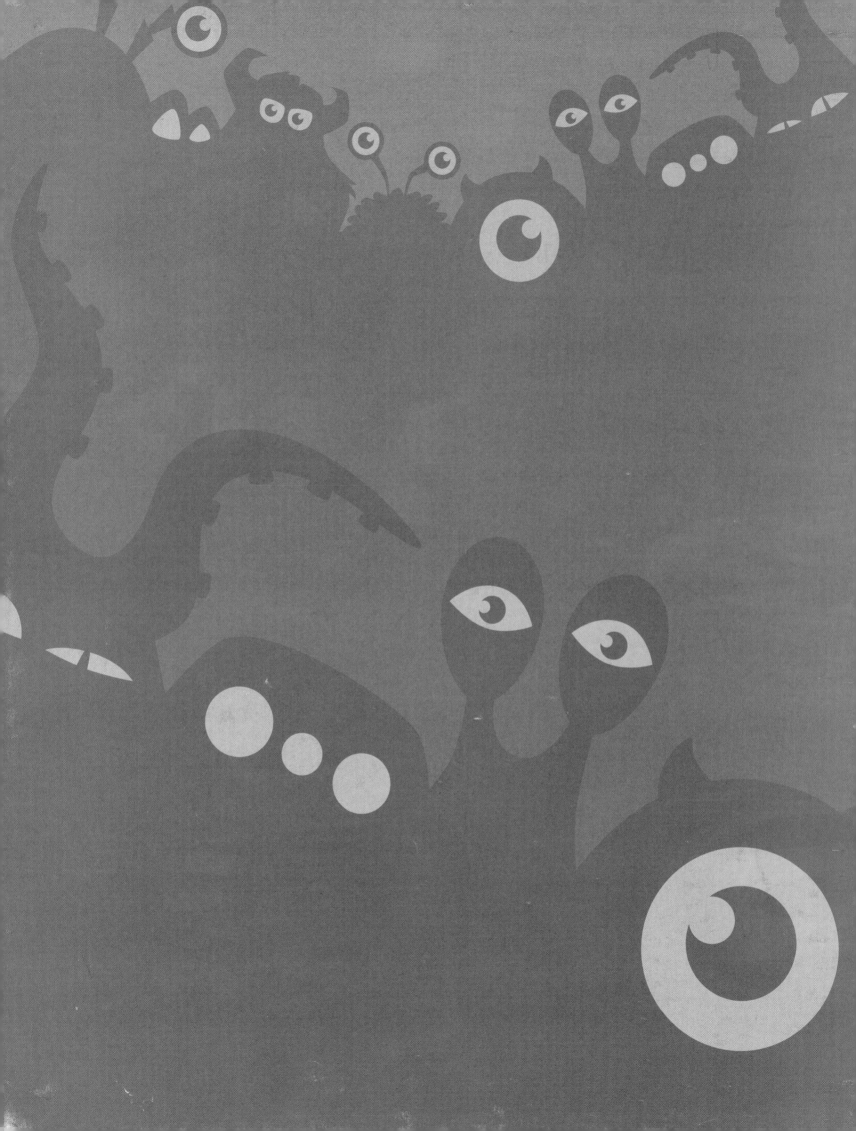